THE LAST TEMPTATION

THE LAST TEMPTATION

GERRIE FERRIS FINGER

FIVE STAR
A part of Gale, Cengage Learning

GALE
CENGAGE Learning·

Detroit • New York • San Francisco • New Haven, Conn • Waterville, Maine • London

GALE
CENGAGE Learning®

LIBRARY OF CONGRESS CATALOGING-IN-PUBLICATION DATA

Finger, Gerrie Ferris.
  The last temptation / Gerrie Ferris Finger. — 1st ed.
    p. cm.
  ISBN 978-1-4328-2589-8 (hardcover) — ISBN 1-4328-2589-5
(hardcover) 1. Custody of children—Fiction. 2. Missing persons—
Fiction. I. Title.
PS3606.I534L37 2012
813'.6—dc23   2012003822

First Edition. First Printing July, 2012.
Published in conjunction with Tekno Books and Ed Gorman.
Find us on Facebook– https://www.facebook.com/FiveStarCengage
Visit our Web site– http://www.gale.cengage.com/fivestar/
Contact Five Star™ Publishing at FiveStar@cengage.com

Printed in Mexico
1 2 3 4 5 6 7 16 15 14 13 12

For my brother, Ron, who has always been my hero.

ONE

Lake was about to dig into his coconut pie when the call came. When it ended, the white flash of his smile ended, too. Thumbing away the small plate and standing, he said, "Looks like another Suburban." He clamped the radio to his belt, dug into his pocket, and threw a twenty on the table. He grabbed his blazer from the back of the chair and clapped his straw fedora over his dark hair. By then, I'd scrambled to my feet and slung my backpack over my shoulder. As we rushed out the door, he asked, "Want to do some scouting, Dru?"

"Sure," I said. "I got a couple of hours before court."

Blues flashing, Lake flew through a yellow-turning-red light, my Saab riding his bumper, my mind ticking off the facts of the first Suburban Girl murder.

A twelve-year-old had been snatched from a sidewalk in Roswell, a lovely old town north of Atlanta. She had been walking home from her private school with two friends. According to them, the white car with blackened windows made two passes. The first time, the driver turned left at a stop sign. The second time, he halted by a curb, slightly ahead of where the children stood beside a water fountain deciding whether to have pizza or tacos. The driver's window slid down, and the victim stepped into the street and walked around to the driver's door. The other kids thought their friend knew him. They thought it was a "him" because the shadowy figure was large enough to fill the driver's seat. As she spoke to him, one of them said the

victim had a smile on her face, but, in the next instant, the door
flung open and their friend disappeared. The girls disagreed on
one crucial point. One said the victim was pulled into the
interior, the other said she dove over the driver. That's eyewit-
nesses for you. Dragged or dove-over, big difference.

The killer dumped the Roswell girl not far from where Lake
braked abruptly to investigate today's dead girl—not far from
where the murderer threw out the second dead girl.

I stayed behind the crime scene tape and watched the uniform
cops and reporters roam the sidewalk. I could see the dump
area, but the ditch fell away from the buckled concrete, and I
couldn't see the body. Two uniforms I know approached Lake
wearing the look of official misery that comes with seeing death
day after day. Reporters show no such misery—only elation for
a byline on the front page. One pumped reporter yelled,
"Another Suburban, Lieutenant?"

Lake—always with a patient face for the press—said, "Just
got here, folks."

I pressed through the throng of gawkers, mentally cursing the
oppressive humidity. My silk blouse clung to my damp skin.
Half the crowd fanned themselves, while the other half wiped
sweat. I scouted faces, looking for a bold murderer. Anyone
who could snatch girls in broad daylight might well show up to
watch the aftermath. I didn't see anyone with nervous eye tics,
so I focused on Lake, now talking to a tall black man. The man
nodded to the two young boys, jittering at his side. Lake squat-
ted on his heels to hear what they had to say. When their
animated account turned to shoulder shrugs and finger twist-
ing, Lake rose and shook their hands. He gave a pat to the
black man's back and led the three to the yellow tape.

A uniform held out a box of latex covers. Gloving his hands,
then pulling shapeless booties over his shoes, Lake walked into
the ditch. The weeds came to his knees. He stood for maybe

fifteen seconds looking down before he sat on his heels. I didn't see his hands touch her—they normally wouldn't before the ME got here, but I'd seen them hover over other corpses with a reverence you don't usually see in homicide cops. Standing, his fists on his hips, he looked at the sky for a long moment. Then he turned and looked at me. I could read his mind. He had a little girl . . . In a few years, she'd be the age of this young dead girl.

The medical examiner's wagon drove up. The uniforms parted the crowd, and the van went into reverse. Voices trilled on the nervous air. A body soon would emerge.

Lake came to me, his shoulders thrown wide as if drawing back from what he'd seen. He pointed to his left. "She was found by those two boys walking home from the convenience store. One of the boys' candy wrapper flew near the body. They saw her gym shirt and that she was a white girl."

"The usual?"

"It appears. Nude below the waist. A garrote around her neck."

"I'm going cruising," I said, then cocked my head toward the gathering of people. "No one in that crowd looked like they were about to have an orgasm."

He started to say something, but I was away before he could protest.

The Saab's air conditioner might as well have tried to cool hell. Driving the narrow streets running off Memorial Drive, a low-to-no-income neighborhood, I saw rusting cars and basketball hoops but little grass. I saw people enduring poverty and despair, but no one with the energy to murder. Back on Memorial, I came to Oakland Cemetery. Soaring monuments rose above the cemetery's stone walls. My daddy was buried there—where elaborate funerary art was meant to console the bereaved. It worked . . . sometimes.

I circled the cemetery again. Across Memorial, I spotted a white Cadillac nose up to a stop sign on Crown Avenue, a street I'd just been down. The newish car stood out against the kudzu vine that climbed the stop sign. I made a quiet left onto the broad boulevard and drove toward Crown. The Caddy's windows were darker than the law allowed, but I could see a big outline behind the wheel and that his head was twisted toward the ME's wagon. When I crept a right onto narrow Crown Avenue, my bumper missed the Caddy's by a foot. A flash came from the driver's left hand, like a diamond in a ring, as his head whipped toward me. Sunglasses. White man. Hefty. Not young. Not old. Hair light—gray or blond. Clothes—red predominant.

I'd blocked his turn left, so he peeled right onto Memorial, into oncoming traffic, toward the cops and the spectators. People screamed; brakes shrieked. Two uniforms raced to squad cars, one shouting into his collar radio.

I got turned around and pulled up behind Lake's car. Two more squad cars came screaming down Memorial. "You get a tag?" Lake yelled.

"Never got a chance," I said, halting beside him. "White guy. Diamond ring. Light hair. Red shirt."

Lake whirled and yelled at a detective. "Banner!" The detective raised a hand like a kid in school. "You get a tag on that Caddy?"

"All but the last two, Lieutenant—three, six, three, dash, two, something, something."

"Call it in, take a couple of officers, talk to people. See if anybody knows or has seen that car or the driver." He looked at me. "Describe him for Banner."

I did the best I could, recalling large ears, too. Banner led two uniforms away, parting the crowd. Lake put his hand on my arm. "First lunch, now looks like dinner will be a wash."

"Can't be helped," I said and wondered what I would have

said had I not been an investigator, too. "I'm off to the courthouse now. Can't keep the judge waiting."

"If I can't get a dinner break, will you go on to my place? I'll be home as soon as I can. There's half a cake in the fridge."

He knows I don't eat sweets. "You just bought the cake yesterday."

His eyes held mine for as long as they could with his colleagues looking on. The he gave me a pat on the cheek like I was a puppy. "And leave some Blue Sapphire for me."

"Better hurry." I do drink gin.

Bradley Dewart Whitney strode into the small room adjoining the judge's chamber like he'd come through the curtain on a catwalk to model his expensive summer suit. I expected him to swirl; he had that kind of narrow-eyed smirk. If it wasn't for his tanned forehead being too high, he would have been *GQ* perfect. He hadn't spared his bucks on hairdressers, either. He was layered and highlighted, blond and artfully tousled. I resisted the impulse to brush back my own brown strands, which hadn't seen scissors in six months.

A gleam grew in his gray eyes. I'd given him the once-over, and, evidently, he thought I liked what I saw.

I got to my feet and stuck out a hand. "Good afternoon, Mr. Whitney." I'm nearly six feet tall, and he was a little shorter.

His fingers brushed my palm. "Good afternoon to you, Moriah Dru." He pursed his lips and laid a forefinger in the cleft of his chin. "Dru is an abbreviated form of Druaidh—the ancient Druid priesthood—the guardians of the old faith."

Did he have this knowledge filed in his brain, or had he done research on me? I said, "Daddy never told me that."

He pointed the forefinger toward the ceiling. "Ah, but you're a descendant, Miss Dru—it's apparent in your fair skin and shining blue eyes."

Usually, I tell anxious new clients to call me Dru, but I didn't see much anxiety in him. "Have a seat, Mr. Whitney."

Before he sat, he looked at the chair as if it had cooties on it. Why the word *cooties* came to mind is a mystery because I don't deal much with children. I work with parents or guardians because their kids are long gone.

He sat and folded one knee over the other, then plucked at the crease of his pants to make sure it hung freely down his leg. He shot his shirt cuffs and adjusted his collar. I waited. He could begin whenever he finished his grooming. He flicked at hair falling on his forehead, then leaned forward as if he remembered why he was here. "We are being confidential, are we not?"

"Of course."

"No reporters, no other snoops?"

"Not unless you call the judge a snoop."

His mouth twitched. "We must have her, I suppose."

I picked up the first item in the file, a photograph of a beautiful blonde woman and her look-alike daughter. "I'd like to go over the basics with you." His eyes didn't blink when he nodded. I continued, "Kinley's eight years old. You're her custodial parent. She was visiting her mother, Eileen Cameron, in Palm Springs, California. She was scheduled to come home Sunday afternoon."

"I was picking her up at the airport at four-thirty-five," he said, looking at his Tag Heuer.

At least my Rolex made us even-steven in the watch department. "When did you last talk to your daughter?"

"Saturday, about one," he said. "She couldn't wait to get home."

"Who were the last people to see them—those who might set a time frame for their disappearance?"

"Eileen took Kinley to brunch at the Palm Springs Country

Club at eleven on Saturday. The staff affirmed they were there for about an hour. After that . . . ?" He spread his hands.

"What makes you think your ex-wife kidnapped your daughter?"

"They're both gone, aren't they?"

"Did your ex-wife give you any hints—a forewarning—this might occur?"

"None—although Eileen is unpredictable. Most women are."

Why the deliberate jeer? "Any idea where they could have gone? Family? Friends?"

"No idea. Eileen's family lives in Monroe, about an hour from here. She couldn't stand them, and she thought better of them than I did. She didn't make many friends when we were married. She wasn't the girl-pal type."

"Did she keep up with old school friends?"

"One. Lives in New York. She's a fashion model."

"What's her name?"

"Naomi Blystone."

I made a note and looked over a copy of the Whitney divorce agreement signed five years ago. "Tell me why you got custody of Kinley?"

He raised his chin and looked like he would proudly brand the letter *A* on Hester Prynne's chest. "Eileen's a chronic drug addict. Failed rehab—twice."

I turned a page. "Eileen's second husband is Arlo Cameron—a Hollywood producer and director. I don't know anyone whose face doesn't show up on a movie screen. He a big name?"

"Not in my world."

"Is Eileen in the movies?"

"No one would mistake her for a talent."

"You've moved since you divorced Mrs. Cameron to Ten Country Day Place. Isn't that off West Paces Ferry, right up the road from the governor's mansion?" He nodded. "You still drive a Honda?"

"Yes."

"And make fifty-eight-thousand a year as an associate at Curriculum Paradigms, Inc.?"

He steepled his fingers before he answered. "I've gotten raises since the divorce."

"How much?"

"I'm not compelled to tell you, am I?"

He wasn't, but something wasn't adding up on this girl's paradigm. "Any other income?"

He raised his eyes toward the ceiling as if dealing with a twit. "I'm also a professor of urban education at Georgia State University. I have a PhD in educational equivalency from that institution."

"Okay," I said. "The Palm Springs PD took Arlo Cameron's statement and passed it along to the Atlanta PD. Cameron says he was in LA for a big show-biz party Saturday evening, and that he came home Sunday afternoon. His wife's car was gone, as was she. He assumed that his stepdaughter was on the plane to Atlanta."

Whitney's hand curled into a fist "I'd prefer that you not refer to my daughter as his stepdaughter. It's an abomination. And don't you, for one moment, believe him. He most certainly helped Eileen kidnap Kinley."

"But why would he risk his career and reputation to hide another man's child?"

"My daughter is a pretty girl." He paused to let that sink in. "I know this isn't your first rodeo."

. He was right. I'm a hundred times more familiar with molestation than I'd like to be. But not all stepfathers are the bastards natural fathers think they are.

Finally, we got around to signing the necessary papers, him

giving me the authority that I needed to investigate the disappearance of his daughter, and me agreeing to work for the sum of twenty-five thousand dollars, not to exceed five days. The expenses were to be negotiated with the court.

"Time to see the judge," I said, rising.

"My favorite bird," he sneered. "The Hawk."

Two

After I quit the Atlanta Police Department, I started Child Trace, Inc. Eight-five percent of my work comes from contracts with the state's public safety agencies—mostly from the apprehension division of the juvenile justice system. It pays my fees and expenses to find kids who've disappeared from foster or custodial homes. When I'm hired by a private citizen, naturally the client pays. The Kinley Whitney case fell into both categories because of an ongoing custody battle between Eileen Cameron and Bradley Whitney.

The juvenile judge put Whitney in contact with me when he requested that the disappearance of his daughter be investigated without the press fanfare that comes with rich people behaving badly. Nonetheless, he thought that the state should pay my travel and incidental expenses.

The juvenile judge, Portia Devon, thought differently.

Whitney whipped out his checkbook and propped it open on the shelf of the witness stand. After he wrote the advance-on-expenses check, he waved it at her. "This is payment for finding my daughter and for keeping the matter private, right, Judge?"

Judge Devon's eyes were like black stones, and when she didn't answer him, he dug the hole deeper. "I don't want a reporter within a mile of me, much less have one shove a camera in my face. I don't want Kinley's and Eileen's pictures on milk cartons and mail box leaflets."

"Mr. Whitney, this is juvenile court—not a newsroom, nor a

police station. My duty is clear. You'll have to negotiate your privacy issues with those agencies." She looked at me. "See me in my chambers."

Folding his arms, Whitney turned to me. "Judges really say that?"

"A lot," I said, watching the judge sweep away, her robe billowing with annoyance.

When the door behind Portia closed, Whitney said, "That ball buster would have given Kinley to Eileen if she could have."

"She's tough, and, like me, she's been to a lot of rodeos."

He folded his arms across his chest and let his head tilt sideways. "I don't think I should like what you're implying. My conduct has been, and is, above reproach."

Could I tell a client to go to hell within an hour of meeting him? Temptation seethed.

I said, "I'm glad to hear that, Mr. Whitney, because when I investigate a case like this, I investigate everyone—back to the time they were in diapers."

His right eyebrow shot up. "Then I'll get my money's worth out of you, Miss Moriah Dru."

"Indeed, you will," I said, snapping the check with a forefinger. I turned to go.

He ran to catch up. "Hey, look, I'm sorry." He spread his arms wide. "This is a tough time. I'm the good guy, remember?"

I nodded without smiling, and we went our separate ways— him out of the courtroom, and me past the bench toward the door into Portia's chamber. I congratulated myself that I hadn't looked back to get a look at his gliding movements in the stylish clothes. Earlier, I'd seen his shoes. They were hundred-dollar wingtip tassels. A man of contradictions.

Portia Devon and I go back to second grade at Christ the King Catholic School. I don't know why I thought of that right now.

Perhaps because she was sitting behind her desk in the cluttered chamber, smoking a cigarette that was clasped in a short, black and gold holder. Cigarette smoking had been forbidden in government offices for years now, so maybe that was why I thought of our school days. Forbidden smoking. I remember in sixth grade, gagging my way through half a pack a week.

I unloaded my laptop and briefcase on the floor and sat in a chair facing Portia. Another puff, and she stubbed the cigarette. "You don't smoke any longer, do you Moriah?"

It was a rhetorical question, and I answered the same as always. "I still don't know what to do with my fists, now that I don't cough any more."

Portia's lip twitched. She was a thin, nervous woman. Her eyes were set so close together they looked like they had been sliced apart by her scythe of a nose. Before her elevation to the bench, she'd been a state prosecutor—one of those no-plea-deals-from-this-office barracudas.

"What do you think of Whitney?" she asked.

"First impressions can be misleading, can't they?"

"A disagreeable Ken doll," she said, rising abruptly. She picked up a bunch of case files representing her morning calendar.

I grinned. "What do you know about Ken dolls?"

"My son has two bedrooms full of dolls. I know every one." It was easy to forget that Portia had been married. It was a brief marriage, and I was reminded for the millionth time why I, at thirty-three, had never married. Five years ago my cop fiancé had been murdered in a drive-by shooting while handing out Big Brothers/Big Sisters leaflets in a neighborhood of warring drug dealers.

Swallowing the unhappy reminder, I asked, "What can you tell me about the Whitneys' custody problems?"

"Not much," she said, plunking the files into her clerk's file bin. "You're not an officer of the court. Juvenile files are confidential."

"You can tell me if you've investigated him, can't you?"

Returning to her chair, she settled in, then answered, "Eileen's attorney took depositions; we heard testimony."

"I'm curious about his wealth. Where'd it come from?"

"All he had to prove to this court was that he had sufficient income, and the good credit and character to take care of his daughter. He's an educator, and he wasn't paying alimony."

"C'mon, Porsh, you can do better."

She fidgeted with her cigarette holder, her mouth drawn in thought. "I can tell you this much. Custody was a typical mudslinging affair. And since he's had custody, Eileen Whitney Cameron has filed eight petitions to get his parental rights terminated. Her last one was . . . well . . ." If a hawk could grin, it would look like Portia. "I have every confidence you'll learn for yourself."

I'd have to be satisfied with that. "I plan on paying a surprise visit to Eileen Cameron's family in Monroe after I leave here. No love lost between Whitney and his ex-in-laws."

"Nor Whitney's ex-in-laws and me. The aunt's a harridan."

"Could Eileen have taken the child there?"

"Not in a million years."

"If you don't want to be found," I said, "the last place on earth they'd expect you to be *is* the place to be."

Portia rose and came to sit in the chair next to me. "Eileen Cameron's mama and daddy are dead. So's an older sister. The family owned a bank. They died in a robbery when Eileen was fifteen. That's when her drug addiction began."

"I take it this harridan aunt had custody of her."

She folded her hands on her lap. "Adele Carter's her name. Adele has a girl of her own. It was a stepmother-stepsister relationship."

"You interviewed Carter?"

"Personally—after she'd given a deposition. She didn't have much good to say about Eileen." She tossed her head, one of her impatient gestures I knew well, and went on, "I wish her words weren't on the record, but they are. The family is fundamentalist Christian with a capital *F*."

"They speak in tongues?"

"I wouldn't be surprised." She leaned forward and put her hand on my arm. "Now you know the drill. Report to me every day. Phone or e-mail."

"Yes, Your Honor." Portia stood, and I bent to pick up my briefcase and laptop from the floor. "Do you think Whitney will pay for my cell minutes and carpal tunnel treatments?"

Portia walked me to the door. She looked up and conveyed that motherly quality even skinny hawkish judges can manage. "Moriah, don't put yourself out on a limb where the son-of-a-bitch can saw it off."

I nodded, feeling the same unease that disturbed Portia's dark eyes.

THREE

Portia went to law school after her bachelor's degree, and I went to community college, then to the Atlanta Police Academy. That career choice had little to do with civic zeal and a lot to do with money, as in: I had none. Daddy was a marginal stockbroker turned insurance salesman. We lived on an edge that was hidden behind Southern gentility, and then one day I realized that Daddy wasn't going to work any longer and that he lay around the house nipping at a quart of Jim Beam or Old Crow. It didn't stop me from loving him, though.

I reached the Saab and threw my things on the back seat. My eight-year-old car was an oven. The mercury had climbed close to a hundred. But that's the South in August.

It was late afternoon, and Atlanta traffic was at its legendary best. Everyone was out of their offices, and on the move, especially on the interstates. But once I got on the Stone Mountain Freeway, heading east, the going smoothed. Monroe, Georgia, is halfway between Atlanta and Athens—the home of the University of Georgia, Portia's alma mater.

Whenever I traveled toward Athens, the same old memories popped up. Even the Whitney case couldn't keep my mind from going back to my affable daddy, who committed suicide when I was a senior in high school.

Before I realized I'd reached the Monroe city limits, I was on Union Street. Monroe is the seat of Walton County. Just to show how my brain lugs around a lot of useless knowledge, I

21

recalled how Monroe got its name and became the Walton County seat. Back about eighteen-fifteen, two plantations—Cow Pens and Spring Place—vied for the site of the county seat. Spring Place won, and to placate the master of Cow Pens, he got to name the city. He named it after Monroe, after the sitting president.

Red brick buildings lined Broad Street, the most prominent being the courthouse with its portico and clock tower. A series of turns brought me to High Prince Road. I made another right. Number 115 was an antebellum gem in need of paint. The black roadside mailbox told me A. Carter lived here. Neat flower beds rimmed the gray wooden porch. I climbed the steps. A hot breeze nudged the white swing hooked to the porch ceiling.

Portia's word came back to me the minute Adele Carter opened the screen door and wiped her hands on her apron. *Harridan.* Her gash of a mouth didn't smile, but she nodded briefly to acknowledge who I was and why I'd come. Her sharp chin moved sideways when she said she had an apple pie ready to come out of the oven. I hurried after her, over a threshold and onto the brick-floor of her kitchen. She pulled the oven door open and stuck a knife in the pie's crust. "Five more minutes," she said, whirling to a counter. She measured cornmeal in a cup and then poured it into a bowl. My impromptu visit, no matter the reason, was *not* going to disrupt her kitchen duties.

I sat at an old chrome table that dated to the 1950s, my nose absorbing hot apples riding on sweltering air. No AC, and the fan oscillating on top of the fridge was losing to the oven. Sweat beaded on my upper lip. My clothes would be soaked when I left, and that might not be for hours since Adele's feisty mannerisms suffered no conversation while she put the cornbread ingredients together. When she went for the buttermilk in the fridge, she brought out a pitcher of lemonade, got a glass, and plunked them in front of me.

With a brusque chin lift, she said, "I've spoke with the police. There's nothing more I can say. Eileen was man-crazy. One was bound to kill her one day." She whipped the batter like she was trying to kill it.

I kept my face impassive. "I haven't heard anything to suggest—"

"That Hollywood gigolo ain't talking the truth."

"You think Arlo Cameron killed her?"

"Either him or that slinky first husband of hers. Son of the devil. Satan shined out of his eyes ever time he looked at me."

"What about Kinley? You can't think—"

"A pawn," she said, slathering Crisco inside an iron skillet. "That's all she was. Poor li'l Kinley. Never went to Sunday school a day in her life."

"Was Eileen raised in Sunday school?"

"I saw to it she was, after her family was shot dead. Money heathens, they were. Went to the country club of a Sunday morning instead of services."

"How did Eileen take to Sunday school?" As if I had to ask.

"Snuck out, if I didn't keep an eye on her." She poured the batter into the skillet. "Went off in the woods with the boys." She smoothed the batter with a wooden spoon. Taking the pie out of the oven, Adele Carter said, "Give you some, 'cept it's too hot." Then she slid the cornbread pan over the oven rack and slammed the door.

"Thanks anyway," I said, finishing my second glass of too-sweet lemonade.

"They all spoiled Eileen rotten," she said, flipping a timer. "Pretty is as pretty does. You don't give in to pretty's every whim."

"Nommmm," I murmured.

"Money. That's all their daddy thought about."

"Well, he owned a bank—"

"I thought Eileen'd never stop crying when they was killed," she said, planting her bony hands on her hips. "The day she stopped, she never cried again. Wish she had of. Drugs got hold of her."

"Do you have any idea where Eileen would go with Kinley?"

"Nary one."

"Would she go to a women's shelter?"

"She'd go to hell first. She's too in love with herself and all her fine things."

"I have to ask you this right out, and no offense . . ." She stood straighter—as if prepared for an onslaught. "Have you, or anyone in the family—her cousin, for instance—heard from Eileen since she disappeared?"

Flashing angry eyes, she said, "I would have told the police if we had."

"If you hear from her in the future, will you call me?"

"You don't have to ask that." She went to the kitchen sink.

I slipped the business card in my hand onto the table. "I'd like your word."

She pushed the faucet tap roughly. "I would be the last person Eileen would ask for help."

"You're family."

She flipped the water from her hands and grabbed a towel. "The bank wasn't solvent. It wasn't my fault."

"Did Eileen's parents leave a will?"

"They did. I was made her legal guardian."

I got it. "Did the court appoint a guardian *ad litem,* too?"

She snapped the towel and nearly shouted, "There was *no money.* The bank wasn't solvent. It made bad loans and lost customers to big banks come to town."

"Did Eileen think you'd kept money that belonged to her?"

She rushed out, into the hall, expecting me to follow. I did.

She opened the screen door and stood back. Once I was through it, she tried to slam it. But I straightened my arm against it. She pushed, but I'm stronger. She drew back, and for several moments we stared at one another. I wasn't going to break eye contact until she did. When she did, she looked past my shoulder.

"Sit on the swing with me for a moment," I said.

Her face tightened into a mask of restraint, and she stared into my eyes. I braced for the punch, but she backed away and stepped onto the porch. Her heavy shoes clomped to the double-seat swing. She sat firm and folded her hands on her lap.

I lowered myself next to her and waited while the swing rocked itself quiet. Placing a hand on her arm, I said, "You loved Eileen, didn't you?"

Tears pooled at the corner of her eyes. She shook her head. "I couldn't—I couldn't—I didn't take her money—there wasn't any left." Her watery blue eyes looked out from raw sockets. "She didn't believe me."

"She was fifteen," I said. "No one could influence her any longer. You could only be her caretaker and watch whatever happened."

She rolled her thumbs against one another. "I did my best." She looked out across her lawn. "I wanted her to—to—*mind* me."

I was certain she wanted to say, "to *love* me."

Some people just can't.

A combination of police training and instinct had me studying the car that followed me down Broad Street, through some turns and onto Highway 78. It was a dark blue Chevy Caprice, less than three years old, no front tag. The person driving wore a cap and had broad shoulders. Man or mannish woman.

At a stop sign in Snellville, he was three cars back. I got off

25

78 at Mountain Industrial. So did he. I turned right on Ponce de Leon. So did he. I was going out of my way to get downtown, and he had to know I knew he was following me.

So what was the point? Intimidation? But by whom, and why? Did those God-fearing relatives of Eileen's have something to hide after all?

But they hadn't known I was coming to Monroe, and Adele Carter hadn't made a phone call while I was there. So how could they get a tail going so quickly?

Whitney's smarmy face came to mind, but I was certain Whitney wasn't driving.

FOUR

When I made a left onto Peachtree Street, the Chevy Caprice went straight across the broad main drag and disappeared down a hill. Good riddance, I thought, and maybe he wasn't following me. I streamed on downtown when my cell played Mozart. Lake. I adjusted my ear bud and answered. Lake said he could take a break for supper.

I turned off Peachtree onto Marietta—a schizoid of a street. Short skyscrapers housed banks and shops and cafés. Going west, I passed the newspaper building, Centennial Park, CNN, and the Omni Hotel. After that, things got shady fast. Now hundred-year-old warehouses flanked the street. During my last year on the force, in a cotton warehouse, six gamblers holding cards had been shot dead. Down the street, a shoot-out at a motorcycle fix-it shop killed one of my APD colleagues. But the street was going trendy, too, with its chi-chi inner-city restaurants. I parked around back of one of them, next to Lake's unmarked squad car.

Il Vesuvio's brick façade was painted to look like a post card from Italy—boats bobbed at a wharf with a towering mountain in the background. Burglar bars covered the stained glass of the entry door. One of the leaded panes had a neat round hole in it. I slipped inside the small vestibule, then into the bar area.

Ah, the smell of Italian floating on air-conditioning.

Lake sat on a bar stool, one hand jingling change in the pocket of his chinos while he gabbed with the bartender. Lake's

27

shirt was a dark blue, no-designer polo knit. When he saw me, he grinned and said, "Dru." When we worked together our last names—M DRU and R LAKE—became our first names. Only old friends like Portia called me Moriah.

Joey the barkeep pulled at a tap and said with a smile, "Officer Dru." He'd never mentally accepted my resignation from the APD.

I gave my ex-partner a brief kiss on the cheek.

"You can do better than that," Lake said, threading his fingers in mine.

Winking at Joey, I rubbed my nose on Lake's cheek and made my alto voice very husky. "Later."

"Tonight sounds like your lucky night, Rick," Joey said, for the millionth time.

A year after my fiancé was murdered, Richard "Rick" Lake and I were assigned to patrol Zone Two. It was a good thing and a bad thing. The good thing was we liked each other and became lovers too fast for our own good. The bad thing (for me) was he got a promotion to homicide, and I didn't like my new partners. They thought they should be able to take Lake's place in my bed, too. Naturally, I bitched to Portia, who was a sucker when it came to old, unhappy friends. She called one day with an idea. "You always liked working with children." My spirit rose. From the time I was eleven, I was the neighborhood babysitter. I adored every one of those kids. Anyway, Portia's call instigated a new career.

Lake's voice brought me back to Il Vesuvio's. "How's the new client?"

"Bad beginning," I said, catching the Amstel Light Joey slid down the bar.

Lake signaled for another Sam Adams, then said, "I ran into Portia when I went to get a warrant. She said her money's on you when the crap starts flying between you and the Ken doll."

28

He grinned and pushed back wisps of black hair hanging on his forehead. His face is all angles and irregularities that blend into one delectable whole. "Rick," as the lady cops and women of the esteemed press so oozingly call him, has a groupie following. Portia would have been one if Portia ever stooped to groupiedom.

"What's up with the Suburban Girls' case?" I asked. His eyelids quivered over his dark eyes and he shook his head. "Anything on the Cadillac?"

"Not yet," he said, fidgeting his hands around his beer bottle. "The computer is humming on the quadrillion combinations."

"When was the Suburban dumped?" I used the word *Suburban* to stay detached, but I still swallowed some water forming in my throat.

"After eight this morning," Lake said. "It stopped raining around then. She left home for swimming practice at seven. At least we know one asshole is doing the murders, no copycats— yet."

There's always copycats in a city like Atlanta. "You giving out particulars?"

"Only to sweet faces like yours," he said, sending my heart into orbit. He went on, "She's from Dunwoody. Thirteen years old. Dad's a traveling man, on his way home from San Francisco. Her mother passed away last year. Rich folks. She had a nanny. Didn't arrive home after the swim session. The nanny called the county police. Amber alert put out on the Caddy. Killer's got the same MO. Kidnap in the 'burbs, dump in the city."

I worried about the fret lines around his eyes, because I knew he was thinking of his own little girl. I heard a noise like static behind me and turned the barstool. Mia, the restaurant owner, stood waiting for us to notice her. She asked, "You ready to eat?"

Gerrie Ferris Finger

"What's for dessert?" Lake asked.

The man and his sweet tooth.

Mia said, "Spumoni and a nice almond chocolate crème brûlée."

"One of each," Lake said. We slipped off the barstools and took our beers into the narrow, low-lit dining room. Our heels clicked across the black-lacquered concrete floor, past fantastic wall murals painted by starving artists for free meals.

We ordered. Me, the light and fantastic veal parmigiana; Lake, the loaded pizza.

"Was the drive to Monroe useful?" he asked.

"I think so," I answered, then drank from my beer bottle. "Eileen and Kinley are definitely not hiding out there." I decided not to tell him about the Chevy Caprice, since he liked to worry about me. I said, "I need to know a whole lot more than I do about Bradley Dewart Whitney."

"What have you and Portia got against this poor man?"

"He is definitely not a poor man. Portia shares my odd feelings about this case. How did he influence his ex-wife's decision to flee, if she did flee?"

"*If?* Any reason to think she didn't?"

Adele Carter's words came back, but I hesitated about bringing homicide into the case with a homicide expert sitting beside me. "The FBI and the local law confirm they're gone."

"Why did you hesitate?"

"Whitney rankles," I said. "Maybe it's the academic looking and living too rich. He's secretive about money and tight as the proverbial tick. He's also arrogant because he's *an academic*. But, unlike most academics, he's too concerned about his appearance and what others think."

"You forgot to mention concern for his daughter."

"It's there somewhere, I suppose."

Mia set wine balloons in front of us and poured the Chianti

30

Reserve she'd let breathe for ten minutes.

After she went into the kitchen, Lake looked at me like he knew what I was about to ask. His chin went down, and the dark in his eyes nearly touched his lashes. "Do you know how many children are kidnapped by the noncustodial parent?"

I made a big show of rolling my eyes. I lived in the knowledge.

As I knew he would, he gave me his I-give-in smile. "I'll look into him. I have nothing else to do these days."

The urge to kiss him was never far from my lips. I reached over and caressed his cheek with one hand and batted my eyelashes like a good Southern belle. "Ah'm evah grateful."

"Where's he live?" he asked, taking my hand and squeezing.

"Off West Paces. Ten Old Country Place."

His low whistle rippled on the air. "What kind of academic is this guy? Stock market guru?"

"A college professor. A curriculum specialist."

"How old's he?"

"Thirty-fivish."

"He inherit, or rob a bank?"

"That's what you're going to find out."

"Okay, so we got this thirty-fivish academic who lives on multimillionaire's row, whose girl has not been sent home from Palm Springs." His eyes livened. "Any chance for a trip?" He was partial to places where he could climb steep, dangerous rocks.

"If the PSPD doesn't come up with Mrs. Cameron and her daughter soon, I'll be off to the desert. I've left messages at the PS cop station and at the FBI bureau there. No one's returned my calls. I hope they'll let me into their territory." I twisted my mouth as if a notion struck. "You got plenty of time off owed you. Come with me, grease me in."

"Then for sure, they wouldn't let you near the city limits."

I grinned, because a bona fide male police officer invaded

territory, while a female, state-contracted investigator didn't.

His cell went off. It makes the craziest noises, like a squirrel shrieking through too many nuts. He waved a hand, not bothering to take it from its holster on his waistband. "Foof it," he said, and I grinned. He was trying to tone down the profanity because his daughter was five and lived with him every other weekend.

The cell continued to shriek. He checked the number. "Shit."

"Duty calling?"

He flipped it open, listened for ten seconds, then pressed END. He looked into my eyes. "The father of the dead girl just got back in town. I hate this work I'm in."

Lake signaled Mia and threw a wad of bills on the table. Outside, the evening heat walloped me in the face. We hurried over broken bricks to the parking lot. At my car, I wrapped my arms around his waist and looked into his eyes. "Put your feelings in a box and shut the lid tight. Isn't that what they taught us at the Academy?"

"Sure," he said, kissing my forehead. "I do it about as good as you do."

FIVE

Lake lives on Castleberry Hill. The old cotton warehouse is two blocks from the railroad yards that split Atlanta north from south. Back when the city was a rail depot in the wilderness, they called it Terminus. As the population grew, the citizens didn't cotton to the name. A doting father renamed the city Marthasville, after his daughter. That name didn't quite capture the imaginations of townspeople, either, and, a couple of years later, a railroad engineer suggested the name Atlanta. The fabled name stuck.

I turned on Peters Street. Most of the warehouses, like the John Deere I passed, had been gutted and rebuilt as high-priced lofts going for almost a million. The cotton warehouse of my destination was not one of those. It, like Lake, lived in the raw.

I parked the Saab in the visitor's parking lot across the street and gathered my brief case, laptop, running shoes, sweater, and whatever else I valued, and left the car unlocked. Bad idea to lock it. The homeless broke windows if they couldn't jimmy them. Not to steal the car, but to sleep in it.

Crossing the street, I looked up at the third story. The high, double-hung windows were raised from the bottom. Green curtains flapped out. "No AC tonight," I grumbled. I wondered if Lake's feelings would be hurt if I went home to my cottage where the air conditioner was as faithful as my homeless cat, Mr. Brown. But in the next instant, Lake's captivating face rose in my mind and my pulse picked up. A knot tightened deep down. No going home tonight. Too edgy.

My head brushed the cord that hung from one of Lake's windows. His doorbell was an old clanger that he'd mounted on a curtain bracket. He also had a mirror set up where he could see the street and anyone standing where I stood on the single-step stoop, now in the act of unlocking the wide loading door.

Inside the stifling hall, the mail was piled on a table made from concrete blocks and boards. Laboring up the narrow, steep steps to the beat of live rap music, my spirit lifted. One of Lake's neighbors was a damn fine photographer and a so-so rapper. We all have our ways of relaxing.

Inside Lake's tin-ceilinged loft, I flipped on the big fans mounted at the four corners of the enormous interior. They remind me of an airplane taking off. The bathroom in the corner is the only lath and plaster room in the place. Divided lengthwise by an oriental carpet running over the heart pine floor, moveable screens separate the other "rooms." In the sitting area, leather sofas and chairs crouch around a stone coffee table. Lake had mounted a big-screen HDTV on the brick wall. I never saw it on unless Susanna, Lake's daughter, was visiting. Susanna has her own partitioned room across from the sitting room. Her mama isn't happy that her precious lives in a loft two days out of twelve, but Suze loves the place, especially the two cats that keep the rats away

I carried my things around a carved wooden screen and plopped my briefcase onto an old commander's chair. My laptop went onto the rolltop desk next to a window. Between the window and the fans, it gets pretty breezy, so Lake weighs his blow-away-ables with crystalline rocks he's collected on climbing expeditions.

In the bedroom, the king-sized mattress and box springs are too big for the old brass headboard, and, like it, the chiffoniers and chests are antiques. Lake and I finally completed their refinishing a couple of months ago.

The place wasn't cooling down, and I fanned myself with an old funeral home fan. The temperature didn't inspire work, and a strange current in the air caused me to go to the window. The city was dark, the moon just a sliver, the streets stone empty. A Coca-Cola sign—a huge Coke bottle cap mounted on a pole—turned and flashed every ten seconds. Why did it make me think of Whitney? He hadn't been garish. He'd been smug and unctuous. With the next flash of the Coke sign, I heard myself whisper into the night. *He doesn't matter. It's the child.*

My mind drifted back to that summer day when I was sixteen and working in our garden. I heard a sharp cry. Dropping the hoe, I lit out for the swimming pool three houses down. The boy went under with what looked like the last gasp. The next few minutes are a blur in my memory, but I'll always think of the man he grew into. We have dinner at least once a year. I pray he outlives me; I don't think I could stand it if he didn't.

Boy, I can really sink into melancholia, just wallow around in it. *So surface, girl, get to the Whitney case.*

My first thought was that Kinley was probably in Los Angeles living it up with her mother, who, I suspected, thrilled at being a pain in Bradley Whitney's ass. I'd be.

I waited for the laptop to fire up, then pulled up the telephone numbers in California.

An answering device picked up my first call. "Thank you for calling the Cameron home. We are unable to talk right now. Please leave a message and we will return your call as soon as we can. It would be helpful if you explained the nature of your call."

I thought I'd keep Arlo Cameron guessing. "This is Moriah Dru in Atlanta. Please call me at 404-103-9992." I got the feeling someone at the other end of the line listened, but then my mama said I was born with a caul covering my face, which, she said, gave me a sixth sense and also meant that I would never drown. Knowing that gives me so much comfort.

At the Palm Springs PD, a different duty officer told me that the detective in charge of the Whitney case was out.

I asked, "What's his name?"

"I can't tell you," the telephone cop said, as if I'd asked for his bank account and social security numbers. "Where'd you say you're from?"

I had to back up, sound sweeter. "Down here in Atlanta. It's where a little girl named Kinley Whitney lives." He didn't say anything. "She was visiting her mother in your city. I've been out there. Great place." No response. "She and her mother, whose name is Eileen Cameron, have disappeared." He grunted. "I'm an investigator with Child Trace."

"Child Trace?"

"I'm working for Judge Portia Devon at Juvenile Justice. Please call the Atlanta Police Department. They know me there."

He said, "I'll leave a note for Detective LeRoi to call you."

Any ol' time is fine. "I'd appreciate that very much. Could you please tell me if the mother and child have returned, or been heard from?"

"No, ma'am."

"They haven't returned or been heard from? Or you can't tell me?"

"Neither."

Thanks, jackass.

I told him politely that I appreciated his help.

Six

I'd no sooner gotten to sleep than Lake's land line rang. It jangled three times before his answering machine picked up. His voice said: "Leave a message. I'll get back to you."

The caller said, "Rick, this is Jeannie. Remember me? Frankie's last month? I waited for you to call. I guess you forgot my number. It's 404-089-4232. I'll wait some more. Or I'll be at Frankie's Thursday night."

There hadn't been many calls like that since we became lovers, but whenever they come, I get teeth-gnashing mad. I went to the kitchen, fetched two cubes, poured two fingers of Blue Sapphire, and wondered, *What in hell am I doing in this oven?*

Back in the bedroom, I watched the Coke cap flash and turn and thought about how frustrated I was, and how scorching the room was, and how I was going to make Lake tell me who Jeannie was and why she thought she could call up at all hours of the night, and why she had his unlisted number, and why hadn't he told her about me—us? When I'd worn myself out with that crap, I laid down—knowing I couldn't sleep. But soon, I was dozing.

I woke when Lake lowered himself lightly onto the bed. By the light of the Coke sign, I watched him through half-closed eyes. He had to see the blinking light on his phone, but he didn't play the message. He must have known. . . .

He removed his shoes and socks and then stood and took off his clothes. He eased himself onto the mattress again. Tonight he didn't make little noises that would wake me, and I continued to feign sleep. To hell with him and Jeannie at Frankie's. Besides, it was too beastly hot to make love.

I'm sure the time that elapsed wasn't as long as it seemed, and I sensed Lake knew I was awake. He turned toward me, and I could feel his eyes. They made me burn with a different kind of heat, one that transcended the swelter of the room and Jeannie's phone message. Rolling close to him, my leg touched his. He rose to an elbow and said, "What made you decide?"

"A curable itch."

In the next instant, an explosion rattled the windows and seemed to suck the air from the room. The blast was followed by an unnatural stillness and a light aura. Something started to sizzle, and my ears popped.

"What the hell!" Lake cried.

I shot up knowing it wasn't a blown transformer—a frequent happening here. We bolted to the windows. Across the street, a car blazed. Brilliant flames and white smoke lit the night. "My God," I cried. It was the Saab. "My car."

I grabbed a pair of trousers, jammed my feet into them, and slung my bra around my chest. Where was my shirt? Lake struggled into the clothes he'd abandoned by the bed. He shoved his sockless feet into loafers. Buttoning up, I looked out the window again. People dashed around in a frenzy. Clutching my sneakers, I raced behind Lake, out the door, down the steps two at a time. He shoved through the crowd. Hopping and stopping, I got my feet into my shoes and followed. We got as close to the burning Saab as we could. Past my car, I saw a white car angled oddly in its parking space, but not on fire.

The photographer who lived upstairs ran up. "Lieutenant?" His fearful eyes took up half his face. "Man, there's someone in that car."

Lake looked at me. Stunned, my jaw hung open, my thoughts

going to the homeless souls who slept in the car. I shook my head. Would Thunderbird wine and a cigarette cause this kind of explosion? I said to Lake, "I left it unlocked, like always."

I felt people around me move as one. Like me, excited and anguished, not being able to take our eyes off the hideousness we couldn't put out.

"Tell me exactly what you saw, Lou?" Lake asked the photographer.

The rangy black man said, "Man, I saw the guy hanging out the window when I was crossing the street. I heard something weird, looked back, saw a little light, and then . . ." He spread his hands and flung them up. "Boom."

Sirens screamed closer. A red station wagon braked at the top of the street. Lake shouted and people pushed back to make way for the assistant chief's car. Lake said a few words to the man as he got out of his vehicle. Both men went to the back of the wagon. The assistant chief handed Lake a mask, a metal hat, and a black slicker. At the same time, two red fire engines pulled across the curb. Seconds later, firefighters sprayed chemicals from large extinguishers. Dazzling sparks gave way to white smoke that pushed up into the darkness. A rush of anxiety had my pulse pounding.

Lake and the assistant chief walked to my Saab and looked into the back seat. The crowd held its breath. Lake and the chief backed away, their faces telling the story. A collective groan floated across me. My mind stuck on the homeless I knew by sight and by street name. I'd routed them out of my car in the mornings. Poor souls, most were still drunk from the night before. If they were really bad, I'd get coffee and donuts from down the street. They were sorry derelicts, down on their luck, but they were humans who looked for an occasional kind word. And now one was dead, or maybe two—in my beloved Saab.

My thoughts came back to the scene. Lake and the assistant chief had moved to the other car, the one at an angle to mine. Lake broke away and walked to me. "We found our suspect."

His words seemed irrational. "Suspect?"

"The killer of the Suburban Girls apparently blew himself up in your car."

I had an absurd moment of disassociation. "What?"

He led me to the back of the white Cadillac. The tag read 363-217. I moved to the front of the Caddy. Between it and my Saab lay what looked like the lower half of a manikin dressed in men's pants. A closer look, and I saw the ragged gore near the belt. Funny how you notice things. I noticed the belt had stayed buckled when his legs and lower torso blasted apart from his chest and arms.

Lake said, "Apparently, he was leaning inside the back window to leave you a surprise."

The assistant chief grunted. "Surprise, surprise."

SEVEN

It was noon before I left the cop station for my office. I parked Lake's Acura in the Atlanta Underground space assigned to me. Despite an urgent need to go home and sleep, I shuffled to the elevator. On the fifteenth floor, I entered the vestibule where two empty chairs waited for clients. I couldn't remember if I had appointments. Somehow it didn't matter. I went through the door into the hall and stopped at the office of my part-time assistant.

Dennis "Webdog" Caldwell tapped rapidly on his computer keyboard. Webdog's a twenty-year-old computer science major at Georgia State University. You can look out his window and see the campus sprawled on the streets below. He lives with roommates a few blocks away, but the futon in the corner of his office sees his body more often than his single bed. Obsession is a wonderful thing, I guess. If information he's seeking zings around on a piece of sand, he won't sleep until he's captured it. He's quick to point out that he's a hacker, not a cracker—the difference being that a cracker illegally uses information he obtains while a hacker simply answers the challenges of an open network system. Sure, Web's a genius, but it doesn't take a genius to understand rationalization.

Webdog glanced up. "Hey, Dru, you okay now?"

"Yeah, Web. What's up?"

"That Naomi Blystone—you know, the model friend of Eileen Cameron's?" I nodded. "Well, she was an easy rundown. She's in Europe this year. The blogs say so."

"So Eileen won't be hiding at Naomi's," I said, and started away. I turned back. "Web, you're into movies, aren't you?"

"Used to be."

"Ever hear of a producer-director named Arlo Cameron."

He sat back and looked like his computer brain was sifting information. "Westerns. Some cop flicks."

"Get me a profile. Whatever you can find on him."

"What'd he do?"

"He's Kinley Whitney's stepfather."

"Oh, man, *that* Arlo Cameron. I wondered why his name was familiar when I saw the list of players in this game."

Did I mention Webdog designs computer games?

On down from Webdog's office, I passed the office of my full-time PI, Pearly Sue Ellis. She wore telephone headphones and was talking two-dimes-to-the-nickel at someone who was doubtlessly ear-sore. She's twenty-four, newly married, has a degree in social work, and was pretty enough to wear the crown of Miss Pecan Pie and Miss Tractor Pull when she was in high school. High energy belies the slur of South Georgia in her voice. At this moment, she worked a kidnap case. The father fled, taking his kids to Saudi Arabia.

After listening to twenty seconds of her conversation, I pitied the U. S. State Department person she badgered.

In my office, my phone rang before I got the backpack straps off my shoulders. I looked at the display. Portia.

"Yes, Porsh."

"What the hell happened on Castleberry Hill? The paper says a homeless man got blown up in a Saab. *Your* Saab."

"He wasn't homeless."

"The article said—"

"They were premature. The man was probably placing a bomb in the back seat of my car when the bomb blew up."

"Christ."

"He's not been positively ID'd yet, but the car was registered to a man named McCracken."

"He's not one of your pet bums then?"

"Doubtful."

"Is this about one of your cases?"

"It's Lake's case. Another girl from the 'burbs was killed and dumped."

"I saw Lake on the news last night. So what's the connection to the bomb in your car?"

I walked to the window and looked down at the miniature human beings hurrying like fire ants with an avowed purpose. I hated explaining my actions to nitpickers, even those of whom I am very fond.

"I was at the crime scene with Lake yesterday," I said. "I saw the guy. I saw his Cadillac and his red shirt. He saw me and my car. They found pieces of his red shirt and the girl's ring."

I could feel her shiver down the line. "He followed you?"

Had McCracken been the man in the Chevy Caprice? I told Portia, "Either me or Lake. Lake had just gotten home when it happened."

"Jesus H. Christ."

I continued to stare down into the street. The punishing sun reflected off the cars. The shimmering waves hurt my eyes. I turned from the window and changed the subject. "Adele Carter has a soft spot for Eileen Cameron."

Thrown off the bomb topic, Portia didn't answer right away. Then, she said, "I don't believe it. What's happening in California?"

"I'm phoning and getting no answers. Arlo Cameron hasn't returned my call. The detective in charge of the case hasn't returned my call, either. The FBI guy out there is on vacation. But the FBI guy in Atlanta confirmed that there've been no calls on Eileen's cell phone, nor has she used her credit cards or checkbook."

"When you leaving for Palm Springs?"

"I've booked for one o'clock tomorrow, keeping my fingers crossed that I get local clearance by then."

"Screw 'em. Go anyway. And, don't forget, tap Whitney for every penny." For my wallet's sake, I hope I'm always on the right side of Portia's cases. She asked unexpectedly, "What are you getting around in?"

For a moment I didn't know what she meant. Then it dawned, and a large lump of misery caromed along my chest wall. I said, "The Saab was getting on in years, but it was dear to me." Portia knew that my late fiancé had helped me afford the coveted car. I continued, "The idea that a human being was killed in it makes it worse."

"If he was planting a bomb to kill you, get down on your knees and thank the automotive gods that he killed himself instead."

"That's a comfort, Porsh."

"The Saab's gone. Never to return. What are you doing for wheels?"

"Lake's Acura, until I get back from Palm Springs."

"I got an idea."

Ignoring her, I said, "I'll probably buy another Saab. Used. Get my guys, Dale and Al at ASR, to go over it with a fine tooth—"

"Listen to me." She had my attention. "Granny's car."

"Your granny's car? It's a Bentley."

"Granny hasn't driven it in a year—since the last wreck broke her hip."

"Portia, no. That car—I couldn't afford the hood ornament."

"It's old."

"And worth a fortune."

44

"Hardly. It's been wrecked so many times, I've lost count. It'll give Al and Dale something to work on."

"I wouldn't want anything to happen to it, like the Saab."

"Get one of those steering locking systems. A tracking device."

"How much is the car worth?"

"How much will your insurance company pay for the Saab?"

"Twelve thousand, tops."

"Half that's about right for the Bentley."

"Porsh."

"Take the offer before I change my mind and put it up on blocks."

"I'm thrilled, but—it's not right."

"You and Lake come fetch it when you're through for the day."

How many more times could I protest? But, truthfully, I was beyond thrilled. That car—what memories. Her grandmother used to drive us to school in that car. After Portia turned sixteen, we used to haul hay to the country for her horses. In summers, we'd pack a dozen friends into it and take off for the Chattahoochee River diving rock.

I sputtered, "But—still—but . . ."

I protested to a dead phone line.

EIGHT

Dartagnan LeRoi sounded like a refugee from a Louisiana bayou. But he said he welcomed my coming out to the desert. "Hell," he said, "a fresh set of eyes is always good. Always good. And you can go places I can't."

I hadn't heard from Lake all afternoon, so I left his car in my Underground parking spot and had Webdog drive me to Portia's. As we drove to Ansley Park, where Portia, her son, and her mother lived in a mansion listed on the Register of Historic Homes, Webdog reported on his web search of Arlo Cameron.

"Born in West Texas, a one-stop town called Appleton. Moved to Los Angeles to go to Hollywood High. Studied theater. Married a couple of times. Ladies' man. Young starlets, production assistants, you know the type. Two official kids. First movie, a dud called *Geronimo's Revenge*. Lives in Palm Springs and Hollywood. No police record. He's a semi-mover-and-shaker in the biz. His movies go from real stinkos to pretty good flicks. He's made tons of them."

"No Academy Award nominations?"

"Hardly. He's low budget. His movies star one medium-well-known actor. Like, the guy's almost over the hill, or he's just getting his career out of the soaps or commercials. The rest of the cast is unknowns."

That was the extent of what I learned about one of Adele Carter's prime suspects.

Portia met us barefoot, in a knee-length Bulldog tee shirt. We trailed her up the Gone-with-the-Wind staircase and through the wide halls to her ninety-two-year-old granny's room. My greeting to a woman I'd adored since childhood met a blank stare, and I almost burst into tears. My mother gets like this.

Portia looked at me. Her expression said, *I hope to hell we don't end up like this.* She said, "Let's get the hell out of this depressing room." She lit a cigarette while her granny cackled at our retreating backs. After that, the oppressive summer heat in the back yard was refreshing.

The Devon garage was an old converted carriage house. When Portia yanked the chain and the garage doors rolled into recesses, Webdog went rhapsodic. The stately blue Bentley sparkled in the slanting sunshine. Portia's gardener stood against the wall, a red garage rag in one hand, a can of polish in another.

Web kept saying "wow," and "cool" as his hands glided over the sateen finish.

I said, "I can't take this car."

Portia said, "You better, or you'll have to answer to Ruben here. He's worked his ass off all afternoon."

Ruben nodded his black head. "Yes, ma'am."

We went over the car's features and reviewed the old handbook. "I'm scared to death to drive it," I said.

"Remember, she doesn't drive like your American cars," Portia said. "She hasn't gone over fifty since we were kids."

I gave her a five-hundred-dollar check as a down payment, and we had a whiskey to seal the deal. Suddenly, I'm driving down Peachtree Street in my new old Bentley, doing an easy fifty. I am in love.

My cell phone rang Mozart. The display read Lake. "Where are you?" he asked.

"In my new old Bentley, almost home."

"You drinking this early?"

"Portia sold me her granny's car."

"Her granny's Bentley?" he almost shouted. "God, it still runs? I hoped to never see that car on the road again. Scared the crap out of me every time I saw it coming."

"She's mine," I crowed. "Oh, Lake. She's fabulous."

"If you say so, now make a U-ey. Get to Cheshire Bridge. We're going to The Cloisters."

"My habit's at the dry cleaners."

"No need of it, Sister Dru. It's a men's private dinner club."

"What am I doing going there?"

"You'll see."

"This a strip joint?" This was Cheshire Bridge Road we were talking about.

"Not at all," Lake said. "Very discreet, private and expensive."

"So who'm I going to see?"

"You'll see."

"You're repeating yourself. Besides, my dearest love, I'm very much in need of a long soak in a cool bath. I'm off to Palm Springs tomorrow, and I've got phone calls to make—"

"I'll meet you on the corner of Liddell Street. Tell the chauffeur to drive carefully."

"Wait." Nothing. "Lake." He was gone.

Day was ending and this jaunt with Lake meant another night in his oven of a loft. Oh, well, I could park the Bentley in my Underground spot. Maybe the plants in my cottage could stand another day without fresh water. Mr. Brown, a cat who doesn't belong to me, but depends on me for a meal, can always slaughter more of the neighborhood fauna.

Lake had parked his unmarked in the lot of a gay men's strip club, across from a jack shack called Toys. There were so many message parlors and lingerie shops on Cheshire Bridge, one had to wonder who worked during the day? The Viagra Inns, as Lake called them, turned out a few heart attacks a week.

It was apparent Lake expected me to park and get into his

car, but I shook my head. His mouth made an O, like he realized I might be a little nervous about leaving the Bentley.

I got out. "You drive her," I said, going to the passenger side.

He locked his car and threw a leather case onto the back seat of my new Bentley. He slipped across the seasoned leather to anchor himself under the steering wheel. He adopted an impressive hauteur. "Are you seducing your chauffeur, Milady, being in the front seat and all?"

"My dear Richard," I said, leaning over to rub my hand across his crotch. "We can be naked in the back seat in two minutes."

Lake laughed and pulled me toward him. We kissed, exploring intimate places for a few moments, then parted. A quick grab at pleasure was not our style. I straightened my blouse. He patted the dashboard. "Forty years old, she is, and another day goes by without a drop of sperm contaminating her leather."

Teenage memories flooded in. "Don't be so sure about that."

He pulled onto Cheshire Bridge Road, humming *"It's Raining Men."*

I asked, "Any more on McCracken?"

"Nope."

"Where'd he get the bomb? How'd he find your place last night?" I thought about the Chevy Caprice that followed me from Monroe. I hadn't seen it since.

"You got questions, I got no answers, but give me time."

Half a mile down, we stopped at a light. The sign for Rucker Road was fastened onto a brick building. The road was little more than an alley between two strip malls. It looked as if it ended half a mile down at a line of trees and overgrown shrubs, but Lake coaxed the car between the rhododendrons and old oaks. The vegetation thinned, and we came to an eight-foot iron fence, spiked at the top. The double gates, supported by stone pillars, were locked. Inside, stood a small gatehouse. No one came out. I noticed a speaker phone mounted on one of the stone pillars; on the other hung a mail slot. Cursive lettering read: The Cloisters.

"This place has changed since I was on the beat," I said.

"It's been transformed into an exclusive and elusive men's club." He reached onto the back seat and picked up binoculars. "It's been the subject of a lot of speculation. Zone Two guys keep an eye out."

"Another Gold Club?" I asked. The feds had closed down the notorious strip club and sent some of its owners to jail.

"Well, it's not public like the Gold Club. We don't know what goes on in there—yet."

I scrutinized the house and grounds. Dogwoods, crape myrtles, and oaks standing in a Bermuda lawn hid much of the limestone Georgian house with its four fake columns attached to the façade like guards at Buckingham Palace. "Those half columns are called pilasters," I told Lake.

"I'll try to remember."

Taking his binoculars, I roamed the conjoined circles over the pitched roof with paired chimneys at each end. The windows were double hung. The paneled front door had a decorative crown over it. An obvious addition rose behind the original roofline. I said, "I remember something about this place. Some oddball religious sect bought the house and built that addition. The neighborhood tried to block it so the zealots would leave."

"They did leave, eventually."

Inside the gates, an asphalt avenue split off, winding around each side of the building. Several cars lined the avenue—Beamers, Lexuses, Caddies, a Mercedes, a Rolls. "Hey," I laughed, and patted the Bentley's dash. "We're good to go in."

"Check the Mercedes?" Lake said.

"Yum. A CL Six Hundred. Over a hundred thou."

"It's registered in the name of Bradley Dewart Whitney. Address: Ten Old Country Place, Atlanta, G-A."

Without pause for thought, I said, "You're kidding, right?" I suspected that Lake had a surprise in store, but this was astonishing.

"Your boy is a regular here."

I looked at Lake and feigned a whistle. "Curiouser and curiouser. He didn't own up to the Mercedes yesterday. Said he drove a Honda."

"He probably still has one in his garage."

"How'd you learn about the CL?"

"Zone Two's been tracking the cars coming and going here. Vice has been checking into who owns the joint."

"How long for the present ownership?"

"Year and a half."

"And his name is?"

"It's a twisted tale."

"It always is."

"You know the origin of the property, don't you?" he asked.

"It's in all Atlanta history books. A railroad magnate built the mansion last century. Hosted presidents, senators, rajahs from abroad. But after a few generations, the heirs died out and it fell on hard times. That's when the religiosos moved in."

Lake said, "They sold it about four years ago to a woman named Burchardt, from Albany, New York, for about a mill. Pretty straightforward, huh?"

"You're going to tell me it isn't."

"The Burchardt woman owned a forty-thousand-dollar condo in Albany, but she moved to Miami on South Beach."

"So this Burchardt woman bought this place when she already had a little place in Albany and a gazillion-dollar place on South Beach?"

"Stay with me now. Burchardt doesn't own the property on South Beach. The people who own South Beach—name is Glass—live in Mountain View, Missouri."

"I think you've lost me. Mountain View? A 'burb of Saint Louis or KC?"

"Southern Missouri. Deep in the Ozarks."

"You're going to tell me those folks don't own their property either."

"Ah, but they do. Their place is a cracker box on an unpaved road two miles from a town of about six thousand."

"People living in a cracker box own South Beach?"

"Not any more."

"You better get to the punch line soon. I'm getting edgy."

He laughed. "They're dead. The husband died six months ago. The wife died about two months ago."

"What of?"

"Him in a car crash, over a cliff. She inherits. She dies of some infection. Intestate. No one's come forward so far. The kicker in this is that they were in their late twenties. She was a teacher; he was a bank teller."

I looked at the mansion and saw grief in the eyes of the windows. "Give me an old-fashioned mob job."

"They're passé."

"Does The Cloisters have a liquor license?"

"Good thinking, but nope. The business is an LLC. One owner of record: Manuel P. Strah." He paused briefly. He winked for some reason, then went on, "The registered agent is a man named Robert White. They lease the building."

"What do they declare their business as?"

"They don't have to. It's private. No liquor is sold. No women seen coming and going."

"Does this Strah run the place?" A notion took hold. "Strah? Strah?"

Lake laughed. "Manuel."

"Straw—Manuel. Straw man."

"You're getting slow. I thought you'd get onto it as soon as I said the name."

"Straw parties are illegal."

"So? You can call yourself anything you want."

"Be a front for yourself?"

"Yep."

"But does any of this have to do with Whitney?"

"He's here all the time, when he's not being academic."

"Okay, so maybe *he* owns this strip joint."

"Oh my dear girl. *Men's dinner club.*"

"Whitney owns a joint for a consortium of gentlemen diners? He's an odd duck, but that odd?"

"No proof of ownership yet."

"You said yourself that this club has inspired speculation."

"That's because nobody talks about what goes on. That, in and of itself, is suspicious, and as you are very well aware, the APD's mandate is to familiarize itself with the entire community it serves."

I laughed at the words spoken straight from the handbook, but my brain was whirling. "Owning this place could explain why Whitney doesn't want the disappearance of his ex-wife and daughter publicized."

"Besides being an educator," Lake said.

"The idea of Whitney being Manuel P. Strah is intriguing," I said, and instantly Portia's hawk face popped into my head. "That would give Portia something to think about."

"It's not illegal to own a private men's club."

"Yeah, but something's out of whack. I'll get Webdog digging on this Burchardt."

"Don't bother. She's a schizophrenic, locked up in a swank high-rise for the insane."

My eyes fastened on the silver Mercedes. I could feel Lake's eyes watching me watching it.

"Your client comes here every afternoon," Lake said. "So

does that Roller over there. Media mogul." He pointed at a vehicle. "See that Hummer there? You'll see that guy tonight in a baseball uniform."

"Just like the Gold Club."

"Whoever really owns and runs this place, they've learned from the Gold Club. It proved to be too public for the rich and famous, especially after some big names had to testify."

I shook my head and looked through the windshield at the virgin white building.

The phone on the pillar rang. Despite my saying he shouldn't, Lake got out of the car and answered it.

I heard him say, "Yeah." Pause. "No." Pause. "We got lost." Pause. "We're turning around now."

"Very correct bastard," Lake said, scooting beneath the wheel. "Let's take a look at the homestead of this academic of yours."

"You check his employment yet?"

"He works where he says he works."

"Any progress on the money front?"

"We can't get bank and tax records without a reason, and he's not in trouble."

Why did my mind say: *yet?*

NINE

West Paces Ferry Road is named for a man named Hardy Pace, who came from North Carolina to establish a ferry service across the Chattahoochee River at Fort Peachtree. The Creek Indians called the little settlement Standing Peachtree, and today it is the heart of ritzy Atlanta.

We passed the governor's mansion and cruised on for a half mile. Lake made a left. After two stop signs, he slowed to turn onto Old Country Place Road. You could rightly call Old Country Place the essence of moneyed understatement. The Bentley hugged a ridge for about a quarter of a mile before we saw the first mansion above us. Then Lake had the Bentley racing down a hill and around a curve. His finger pointed left. "A Falcons player lives there."

"Well, it's not all old money then."

"None, if you ask me," Lake said.

We passed several gated driveways. The homes, set back, had privacy fences and hedges to keep the snoopers from ooooh-ing at their opulence. Lake slowed; we'd come to a black mailbox with "10" stenciled in a corner, in very small numbers. Lake stopped. A home security sign was shoved into the ground alongside a sign that said, "Invited Visitors Only." Up the hill, a stone fence came together at iron gates. "This is as far as we go," Lake said, looking thoughtful. "For now."

I looked at him. "Whitney seems to fascinate you."

"When I find out where he gets his money, and if it's legit,

55

I'll lose interest fast."

"I'll be disappointed if he's inherited."

Grinning, Lake said, "You want rotten, baby, I'll do my best to give you rotten. We're checking the public records. Wills, trusts, probate, land deeds."

We turned around in Whitney's narrow driveway, and I wondered irrelevantly how he got up there in an ice storm. As if he'd been on my wave length, Lake said, "Boy doesn't have to worry about the Chattahoochee River flooding."

We'd gotten a hundred yards past Whitney's driveway and started our descent when a silver car sped toward us. The grill was unmistakable. A Mercedes. A sleek CL 600. The Mercedes hugged the yellow line, and the Bentley's right tires spit cracked asphalt as they hit the shoulder. The Mercedes fled past. I turned to see it lurch to a stop and brake lights flash as it backed up. Lake got all four tires back on the road and revved the gas. I was proud of my new old car and kept watch out the back window. "He's still backing up."

"He won't be for long, if he values that car."

I lost sight of him when we rounded a sharp curve.

"Coincidence or what?" I asked, still looking behind me. We were on a straight stretch, descending the hill. Nothing followed.

Lake said. "The trees around The Cloisters have eyes and ears."

We reached West Paces Ferry Road, and Lake's cell screeched. He looked at the screen and punched a button. "Lake," he said, then listened for a second or two. "So what's up, doc?" he asked. I didn't like the look on his face. He said, "Shit!" and punched END.

"What?" I asked.

"Autopsy on a man found dead in back of a churchyard. It's mine, and the ME wants me there."

That meant I was going home to my cottage after all, which secretly delighted me. I looked at my lover with sorrow in my eyes. The sorrow was real, but until he got his AC units up and running again, it was too stifling for love.

"Sorry about that," he said, reaching to clutch my knee and giving it a shake.

I never went to Lake's place on the day he attended an autopsy. It takes a while for the smell of death and formaldehyde to wash out of the skin, or so he thought. He'd scrub himself raw in his primitive shower before he felt alive again.

Then, uninvited, my thoughts strayed to a voice on a recording device. Jeannie. *I'll wait some more. Or I'll be at Frankie's Thursday night.*

Well, at least it wasn't Thursday night.

Ten

On the way home, my cell played Mozart. I had half a mind not to answer. I enjoyed driving the Bentley and watching the people gawk, but I couldn't ignore a client and inserted the ear bud.

"Mr. Whitney," I said. "Did you get my message?"

"Glad you're finally going to Palm Springs. What took so long?"

"I had to get clearance from the authorities there, Mr. Whitney."

"You can call me Bradley. But don't shorten it to Brad, *please.*"

"I call my clients by their last names. It keeps me objective." I turned onto Peachtree Battle. Almost home. Relief was near. Truth to tell, the Bentley's AC wasn't all that great, either.

"I'd rather you be subjective," he said.

"Is the tap in place yet?"

Whitney had agreed to an FBI tap on his home phone in case Eileen or Kinley, or someone connected to them, called. "Yes, and already I've had a few hang-ups this afternoon." Was his voice accusing or was it my imagination?

"Do the numbers mean anything?"

"No. But they're all local. I assume the FBI will track them."

"They will."

"I think someone followed me," he said.

"When was this?"

"You've found out where I live now, haven't you?"

58